NICKELODEON

SpongeBob SquarePants

MY NAME IS CHEESEHEAD

adapted by Erica David
based on the teleplay "Who Bob What Pants?"
by Casey Alexander, Zeus Cervas, and Steven Banks
illustrated by Victoria Miller

Ready-to-Read

Simon Spotlight/Nickelodeon

New York   London   Toronto   Sydney

W9-ARP-035

Stephen Hillenburg

Based on the TV series *SpongeBob SquarePants*® created by Stephen Hillenburg
as seen on Nickelodeon®

SIMON SPOTLIGHT
An imprint of Simon & Schuster Children's Publishing Division
1230 Avenue of the Americas, New York, New York 10020

© 2008 Viacom International Inc. All rights reserved. NICKELODEON, *SpongeBob SquarePants*, and all related titles, logos, and characters
are registered trademarks of Viacom International Inc. All rights reserved, including the right of reproduction in whole or in part in any form.
SIMON SPOTLIGHT, READY-TO-READ, and colophon are registered trademarks of Simon & Schuster, Inc.
Manufactured in the United States of America

4 6 8 10 9 7 5 3
Library of Congress Cataloging-in-Publication Data
David, Erica.
My name is CheeseHead / adapted by Erica David ; based on the teleplay by Steven Banks ; illustrated by Victoria Miller. −1st ed.
p. cm. · (Ready-to-read)
"Based on the TV series SpongeBob SquarePants created by Stephen Hillenburg as seen on Nickelodeon."
ISBN-13: 978-1-4169-6863-4
ISBN-10: 1-4169-6863-6
I. Banks, Steven, 1954- II. Miller, Victoria (Victoria H.), ill. III. SpongeBob SquarePants (Television program) IV. Title.
V. Title: My name is Cheese Head.
PZ7.D28197My 2008
[E]−dc22
2008004304

One day I woke up and found myself
in a strange place.
Where am I? I wondered.
Uh . . . **who** am I?

I had no idea how I got here.
Two friendly people helped me out.
They told me my name was
CheeseHead BrownPants.
CheeseHead BrownPants?
That didn't sound right.

I checked my pockets for clues
to help me remember.
All I found was a bubble wand
and some bubble soap.
Suddenly my new friends screamed
and ran away.

I started walking to look for
some answers.
Soon I arrived in New Kelp City.
The streets were dark and empty.

NEW KELP CITY

items

I bumped into someone by mistake.

"Sorry, sir," I said.

"You are not sorry!" the man cried.

"You were trying to take money
from my pocket!"

"I would never!" I said.

"Yeah, right! If you are looking
for money, get a job!" he said.

I went to look for a job at the bank.
"Mr. BrownPants, you did not
   fill out this form," said the bank lady.
"I know. I can't seem to remember
   anything," I said.
"Do you have any special skills?"
   she asked.

"I can do this!" I said, taking out
my wand. I blew a shiny, soapy bubble.
The lady gasped and told me
to leave!

Luckily I found a job at a
construction site.

"Thanks for the job," I told my boss.

"BrownPants, that hammer is not
moving fast enough!" he shouted.

"Yes, sir!" I replied.

I blew a large bubble and
rode it up the building,
hammering faster
than before.
When my boss saw the
bubble, he yelled,
"BrownPants, you
can't do that here!
You're fired!"

I wandered around New Kelp City,
feeling very sad and lonely.
I didn't understand why everyone
was acting so strangely.
At last I met some people standing
by a fire.

"Hey, do you mind if I blow bubbles?"
I asked. "It will cheer me up."
"You can't do that here!" they said.
"Don't worry," I said, as I took
a deep breath and blew a shiny,
soapy bubble.

Suddenly a street gang appeared.
"Do you have any idea who we are?"
the leader asked.
I shook my head.
"We are the Bubble-Poppin' Boys,"
he said. "Nobody blows bubbles
on our turf!"

"Yeah, **nobody**," his friend said.
"We have ways of dealing with
bubble blowers like you,"
the leader added.

I started to run as fast as I could.
But the Bubble-Poppin' Boys
chased after me!
I had to think of a way to escape.

Suddenly I had an idea.
I blew some bubbles and
climbed them just like stairs.
This made the gang more angry.

Then I blew bubbles shaped
like a raft and an oar.
I paddled away from the
Bubble-Poppin' Boys.
But this time they were ready.
The gang took out slingshots.
They launched pebbles into the air—
and popped my bubble raft!
What was I going to do now?

I took a deep breath and blew
one giant bubble that closed around
the Bubble-Poppin' Boys.
They were trapped!
The bubble floated away
with the Boys inside.

Suddenly everyone ran out
into the street and started to cheer,
"You have freed the city!
Now we can blow bubbles again!"
They were so happy that
they made me the mayor
of New Kelp City!

Later I spoke to the crowd.
"Citizens of New Kelp City," I said,
"I promise you that it will always
be safe to blow bubbles in the streets,
or my name isn't CheeseHead
BrownPants!"

"But your name isn't CheeseHead
   BrownPants. It's SpongeBob
   SquarePants," said a squirrel
   I had never seen before.
"Who are you?" I asked.
   She said her name was Sandy.

"I am your best friend, Patrick,"
said a big pink sea star.
I shook my head.
"SpongeBob, come back with us
to Bikini Bottom," said Sandy.
"It will help you remember."

"I can't. I have an important job
to do as mayor," I said. "In fact
I have a meeting right now."
A boat arrived to take me
to my meeting. But it took me to
Bikini Bottom instead!

"Here it is: the Krusty Krab,"
said Sandy. "You must remember
this place."
"Nope," I replied.

A crab stepped forward.

"SpongeBob, stop kidding and start
   frying up those Patties!" he said.

"I was a fry cook before?" I asked.

"The best," said the crab.

"I am sure being a fry cook
   is great," I said, "but I prefer
   being mayor of a major city."

I began to walk toward the door
when suddenly—*bonk*—
something hit me on the head!
"Ouch!" I cried.
I rubbed my head and looked around.

At that moment my memory came back.

"Hey, I remember this place!" I said.

"SpongeBob's back!" Sandy cheered.

"Hooray!" cried Patrick.

"Into the kitchen SpongeBob,
me boy," said Mr. Krabs.

"I am sorry, Mr. Krabs, but the people of New Kelp City need me," I said.

Just then there was a report on TV. "This just in: New Kelp City is in trouble!" the reporter said.

"The streets are clogged with bubbles!
No one can see where they are going!
Citizens blame Mayor BrownPants
and his new bubble-blowing law."
"Hmm, maybe being mayor
isn't all it's cracked up to be," I said.